Meet Matt and Roxy

written by Karen Huszar

photography by Susan Huszar

ORCA BOOK PUBLISHERS

Hi. My name is Roxy.

This is my best friend, Matt.

Matt and I are pals.

We have been pals forever.

Matt and I do everything together.

We go to the beach…

search for bugs…

and play on the jungle gym.

When it's hot outside, we stay cool in the pool.

Matt can make the biggest bubbles.

One of our favourite games is playing dress-up.

Sometimes we put on costumes and play make-believe.

This is Matt's magic rocket. How can we make it move?

It helps to have a strong head.

When we go for walks, Matt and I look for neat things.

We always find something special to take home.

We love to share ice-cream.

After a fun day, Matt and I relax.

It's bath time. We stay in the tub until our toes are wrinkly.

Hey, what's that under the covers?

It's Matt and me.

Good-night, Matt. I love you.

In loving memory of Roxy

To Dennis, Mattie, Lucas and Lanny
S.H.

To David and Kira
K.H.

Text copyright © 1996 Karen Huszar
Photography copyright © 1996 Susan Huszar

The publisher would like to acknowledge
the ongoing financial support of the Canada Council,
the Department of Canadian Heritage and the British Columbia
Ministry of Small Business, Tourism and Culture.
All rights reserved.

Orca Book Publishers
PO Box 5626, Station B
Victoria, BC V8R 6S4
Canada

Orca Book Publishers
PO Box 468
Custer, WA 98240-0468
USA

Canadian Cataloguing in Publication Data

Huszar, Karen, 1959 –
Meet Matt and Roxy

ISBN 1-55143-055-X (pbk.)

I. Huszar, Susan, 195 –   II. Title.
PS8565.U89M43 1996   jC813'.54   C96–910282–8
PZ7.H96Me 1996

Design by Christine Toller
Printed and bound in Hong Kong

10 9 8 7 6 5 4 3 2 1